I0618766

Little
Lua

Little Lua

Jenefer Savoeung

Life Rattle Press
Toronto, Ontario

Little Lua

Library Archives Canada Cataloguing in Publications

Life Rattle Press New Writers Series
ISSN 1713 8981

First Canadian Edition
ISBN 978-1-989861-32-5

Cover design and typeset by Jenefer Savoeung
Edited by Jessica Gelar

Published in Canada by Life Rattle Press
196 Crawford Street
Toronto, Ontario M6J 2V6
www.liferattle.ca

To my friends, my family, my home.
No one grows alone

—

Contents

Prologue

"Why do fairy tales end after the wedding?" Lillian rested her chin on one arm that dangled out of the car window and caressed her baby belly with the other.

"Is that rhetorical, or…?" her husband, Diego said, glancing at her from the driver's seat.

"What happens after the wedding? What do the lovers do?" Lillian said with a foggy voice.

"Well, it depends on the tale."

Lillian looked out the window. She was six months pregnant and had been bedridden for months. Her legs and back ached when she walked but she needed the fresh air, so Diego suggested a drive. Lillian wanted to look at homes they could not afford. Diego obliged, hoping she would forget.

"Whatever you want, Lillian Lua." Diego grinned.

He liked to say Lillian's new name out loud. His last name with her first name. The Luas. It had been two years since they got married, but it still sounded pleasant to his ears. Lillian and Diego met when they were sixteen and married two years later when they turned eighteen. They would've been married longer if Lillian's older brother Clark hadn't asked her to wait.

They entered a neighbourhood surrounded by trees and black, metal fences. A row of townhouses lined the edge of the street.

"That's a nice one." Lillian pointed to a charming, little home on the corner. It had stone walls, a stained wood door, and rustic hinges. An overgrown garden filled the front yard and ivy climbed the arched windows.

Diego slowed the car down and peered out the window on Lillian's side of the car.

"That is nice," he said.

Lillian rubbed her belly and smiled.

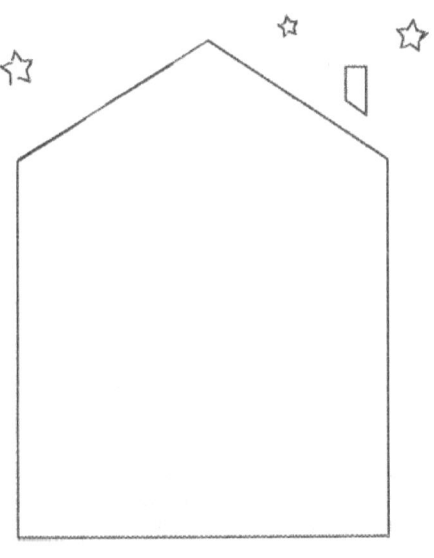

Chapter 1

Welcome to Gaoda

I n a little townhouse in Gaoda, Lillian and Diego Lua set up their dream. They talked about having their own home and family ever since they started dating at eighteen years old, four years ago. It might have been a traditional-sounding dream, but it was something the Luas never had.

Lillian and Diego first met while working at a packaging warehouse as teenagers. Lillian grew up in a small apartment with her grandmother and older brother Clark. Diego, newly immigrated from Mexico, lived between foster homes until he settled in Penna City. When they weren't at high school, Lillian and Diego spent most of their workdays around their middle-aged coworkers who liked to give them advice. Their coworkers would talk about what their lives could have been like in America if they chose the right city to live in. A city like Gaoda.

The warehouse workers praised the small town of Gaoda in northern Minnesota. On lunch breaks, Lillian and Diego, along with their coworkers, would flip through the *New Life* real estate magazines and point out their favourite homes. Lillian and Diego liked the cottage-style bungalows that looked like they belonged in storybooks.

One day, as Lillian and Diego were flipping through the magazine at work, they found an ad on the last page. The ad read, "Gaoda kickstarts small families." Lillian folded and tucked the magazine into her lunch bag.

That night at home, Lillian read up on the town of Gaoda and studied maps and guides. Gaodan families had the chance to live in small townhouses that the pamphlets referred to as starter homes. Next to the townhouses were single homes. Moving further into the city, the homes grow from bungalows to two-storey homes, from one-car to four-car driveways, and from couples to large nuclear families.

The Luas flipped through the magazines often after they found out Lillian was pregnant. They lived with Clark and his apartment started to feel small when they found out they were expecting. The Luas could barely fit a queen-sized bed in the spare room, much less a crib. Even with the windows closed, they could hear the traffic, dog barks, and sirens.

When Clark found Lillian's collection of real estate magazines, he joked that Lillian's pregnancy brain had her craving suburbia. She didn't deny it. She sometimes had Diego drive around the Gaodan region to look at homes for fun. A few of the townhouses had "Grow in Gaoda" and "For Sale" banners on their front lawns.

Clark lost his job when Lillian was six months pregnant. To continue earning an income, he decided to take on travelling photography, so he no longer needed his apartment. Lillian didn't want it either. That weekend, Lillian and Diego drove back to see the townhouses in Gaoda.

★

"It's a step up from an apartment," Diego said when they first walked into their new townhome. It sat on the corner of the street, facing a line of single houses. He stacked up boxes along the staircase and in each room. It took them longer to unpack as they needed to stock up on groceries and baby products when Lillian wasn't bedridden.

Mrs. Anderson was their first visitor. She arrived unannounced, holding up a glass container of stuffed broccoli casserole. Lillian and Diego could not hide the wall of unpacked boxes in the living room.

"It's vegan and very healthy," Mrs. Anderson said as she handed it over.

"Oh." Lillian brushed back her messy hair and reached for the container.

"It means there's no meat," Mrs. Anderson said.

"Yes, thank you." Lillian nodded.

"This is just a custom we have to welcome people to the neighbourhood." Mrs. Anderson smiled.

"I appreciate it," Lillian said.

"May I?" Mrs. Anderson said as she took a step into the Luas' home.

Lillian stepped back as Mrs. Anderson walked in. Her heels clicked on the linoleum tiles. Mrs. Anderson was twenty-seven but dressed like she was much older. She wore a tight blond ponytail, red turtleneck, and chunky black jewels around her neck.

"I just wanted to check in and see how you're settling," she said with a tight-lipped smile. "We're a very giving place."

"Uh, yes, we are still settling in," Lillian replied.

"I see that."

Mrs. Anderson walked into the kitchen while Lillian searched for an empty spot on the countertop to place the casserole.

"We have been a little busy," Lillian said, crossing her arms.

"Of course." Mrs. Anderson stared at Lillian's belly. "Where's the father?"

"He's looking for work."

"Already? The first months with your baby are critical." Mrs. Anderson studied the room.

"Yes, but we should prepare," Lillian responded.

"My husband works a lot too. But with my first son, he cut back on his business trips. Children need their fathers, you know." Mrs. Anderson glanced back at Lillian.

Lillian nodded and followed Mrs. Anderson as she examined the rooms and offered design tips.

"Just because it's a townhouse doesn't mean it can't be well-decorated," Mrs. Anderson said, running her hand along the bright yellow walls.

"Right. We are still settling in. Would you like to sit on the patio in the backyard?"

Lillian offered the patio because it was the cleanest spot of her home. Lillian poured a cup of sweet tea and placed a milk carton, spoon, and a bottle of honey in front of Mrs. Anderson. Mrs. Anderson glanced at it, took one sip, said it tasted lovely, and did not drink more.

Lillian sat back, sipped her tea quietly, and listened to Mrs. Anderson chatter about the spacious parks and high-ranking schools in Gaoda. Sometimes she would stop to say, "does that make sense? Did you understand?" Lillian would try to include a "yes," "wow," or "of course" into her responses.

After Mrs. Anderson left around sundown, Lillian spent the evening cleaning. She put away the boxes and covered the cracks of missing paint spots in the walls with drawings or paintings that they collected and repainted from flea markets. Diego had hung up Clark's surrealist paintings and black-and-white photography on the walls. Lillian did not understand why Diego loved Clark's artwork.

"Clark helps us out so much. We need to support him too," Diego had said.

"All he did was make the picture black and white," Lillian said, crossing her arms. "That's considered art?"

Even the other mothers who visited Lillian pointed out how creative and emotional the artwork looked.

"It must be an expensive artist," one of the neighbours said.

"Not at all," Lillian said.

"He's a new artist," Diego added.

Almost every day, a new neighbour from the neighbourhoods across the street visited the Luas' home. The neighbours were eager for tours and commented that it was a comfy and charming place for a nice, young family. The women offered Lillian old toys and clothes and promised to bring food over while the men talked about how they could help Diego fix up the home. When Lillian refused their donations, they waved their hands and said, "nonsense, we're a giving town." The neighbours' other favourite phrase was "when's the next?" when they watched Lillian pat her stomach. Lillian would glance at a wide-eyed Diego, and they would share a small smile.

★

Lillian and Diego spent their nights preparing their newborn's nursery. They painted the ceiling to look like a starry sky with dark blue paint and speckles of white. They lined the crib with fluffy, white sheets. A messy stack of books stood in the corner of the room. Lillian and Diego arranged and rearranged the book pile as they decide which book they would read to their newborn first.

Lillian sat on the floor browsing Diego's collection. He had a lot of fairy tale books from around the world gifted to him by his foster parents. Lillian's grandmother Yey Chan didn't read her fairy tales, but she recited Southeast Asian ghost stories. Lillian and Clark listened to all her stories, even if they made Lillian nervous to sleep at night. Yey Chan said they didn't have to be scared as long as they protected each other.

In Diego's book *Tales from Asia*, the rough line drawings reminded Lillian of the Japanese horror comics she used to steal from Clark. The horror comics were full of black-and-white illustrations of eerie faces against patterns and spirals.

"Might as well tell ghost stories instead," Lillian said, tracing her finger along a picture of a wooden house with two little kids sitting inside.

"But this is a good one," Diego said, crouching next to Lillian on the floor. He pointed at the last drawing of a little boy and little girl hanging onto a rope, their feet dangling in the air, as a tiger looms around on the ground.

"Look at this." Lillian flipped to the page where the tiger jumps up towards the kids.

"It's a good lesson," Diego said. His straight face softened into a smile. "On having a pure heart."

"Then you will be protected by the sky?" Lillian said.

In the story, two little kids, brother and sister, are in danger of being attacked by a tiger. While trying to escape, they wish for a rope from the sky. If they have pure hearts, they can climb the sturdy rope. If they do not have pure hearts, the rope will rot.

"It's better than falling to the ground," Diego said. He watched Lillian examine the last few scenes where the tiger grabs the rope. It snaps. The tiger lies on the ground with a pool of black ink under it on the next page.

Lillian shook her head and smiled. "I don't know if the black-and-white pictures make it better."

They spent each night in the nursery, flipping through books as neighbours dropped off their own collections of children's books. But the books they received did not seem like the right story for their baby. Lilian and Diego kept going back to the fairy tales. They could not decide on a book until their newborn arrived.

Lillian and Diego named their daughter Maria. Lillian liked the name from a Portuguese fairy tale called *Clever Maria*. Diego joked that it was Lillian's way of asking for a daring daughter like the character.

In the hospital, Maria only opened her eyes for a short moment. Most of the time, her eyes stayed closed, whether it was to sleep or cry. The doctors reassured them it was normal. They said it was "newborn's cry." Lillian and Diego would take turns rocking her whenever a sob began.

When they arrived home from the hospital, Lillian cradled a crying Maria into their townhome. Maria's hoarse hiccups stopped when Lillian and Diego walked into her nursery. Diego turned on the paper lanterns around the room as Lillian laid Maria into her fluffy, white blankets. Maria squinted. Then, in slow blinks, Lillian saw Maria's big, deep brown eyes. Maria examined the reflection of the soft glow of the star decals scattered across the ceiling.

"Her eyes are twinkling." Diego smiled.

"She's taking in the world." Lillian fixed her collar. They could not stop looking at her eyes.

For many nights after they brought her home, they sat at Maria's crib and watched her fall asleep. Diego read into all her movements as if they were signs.

"She could be a dancer," he said when she flailed her hands.

"She's not even on her feet yet," Lillian said.

"Or a fighter! Look at that grip." Diego wagged his finger in front of a wide-eyed Maria. Her little hands balled into fists as she reached up for Diego's finger.

A harsh ringing from their phone snapped Maria out of her trance. Her face scrunched into sobs. Diego slumped back and reached for the phone.

"Are you going to be a singer, *mija*?" Lillian picked up Maria. *Mija* means my daughter in Spanish.

Maria buried her head into Lillian's shoulder, heaving out snot and tears. Diego ran his hands into her hair, already soft and full and always sticking to her often wet face.

"You can be anything, my Maria," he said.

★

Diego started to pick up night shifts over the next few months. He couldn't find work in Gaoda, so he had to work thirty minutes outside of town at another packing warehouse. They let Diego take five months off after Maria was born, but bills and expenses built up, and Maria's diapers and formula ran out quicker than Lillian and Diego expected. Lillian called her brother Clark for help, but he was travelling for his photography work.

Lillian did not see many of the neighbours except for Amy Wilkinson. Amy had short, blonde hair and a babyface, but she was twenty-six and had five-year-old twin girls. When they were at daycare, Amy came by to give Lillian company. Amy always brought a collection of fresh organic fruit from her parents' farmer's market. Amy talked to Lillian about being a young mother and taking care of her twins and how important her husband Scott was in the process.

Lillian appreciated her company and mainly listened as Amy loved to talk. Every time she came to visit, Amy had a new story about her twins, her house, her work, or her husband. She also managed to steer the conversation back to questions about Diego.

"Would Diego do this for you?" Amy would say. "Scott reads to the girls every night. He cooks breakfast too. I just want you to be prepared."

"Diego does his best," Lillian would tell her.

It was easier to calm Maria down with Diego around. Most nights, when Lillian was alone with Maria's wailing, Lillian felt like squeezing her daughter tight. This had made her feel terrible, but Maria's crying grew irritating. Lillian would sit on the floor of Maria's nursery, bouncing Maria on her lap—maybe a little too fast—and mutter, "please calm down."

"It's newborn's cry. Newborn's cry," Lillian told herself.

Eventually, after what would feel like hours, Maria's small whimpers would slow down as she fell asleep. Lillian would rest her head back on the wall and fall asleep with Maria.

Lillian was happy to have Diego home on Sundays. He vowed to always take Sundays off even if he spent his mornings hunched over the dinner table, filling out insurance and tax forms.

One Sunday afternoon, Amy and Mrs. Anderson came by to drop off a basket full of bananas, apples, and peaches.

"They're the best fresh and local fruit," Amy said as she placed the basket on Lillian's dinner table.

"*Es esta local?*" Is this local? Diego asked in Spanish and picked up a banana.

"He says thank you for fresh fruits," Lillian said, turning to Amy.

"*Arigato,*" she replied in Japanese and bowed.

"Uh…*de nada.*" Diego bowed back and glanced at Lillian.

"Was that right?" Amy said. "I wanted you to feel welcome here, so I learned different ways to say thank you in Asian languages."

"Well, yes, my wife is Asian," Diego said. "She's Cambodian and Filipina so she speaks Khmer and Tagalog."

"Oh, but you're…" Amy said, "you have a little accent too."

"Yes, I was born in Mexico," Diego said.

"I've heard Lillian speak Mexican."

"We both know Spanish, yes," Diego said.

He was reminded of why he let Lillian deal with the neighbours. They often mixed up their Hispanic and Southeast Asian identities, commented on Lillian's deeper brown skin, and wondered how they could easily bounce between languages. In the warehouses, Lillian and Diego worked with several bilingual people. Their coworkers did not notice when they spoke a mix of Spanish, Khmer, Tagalog, or English.

"Wow, I barely know my own language." Amy looked at Lillian. "My mom said learning too many languages would take up space in my brain."

"I grew up around many languages," Lillian said.

"Why did you come over?" Diego said, shifting his weight to his other leg.

"We came to ask if you will be at the town meeting dinner?" Mrs. Anderson finally spoke. "You can learn about the town."

"We welcome all families." Amy smiled.

"Well." Lillian glanced at Diego. "We'll be watching Maria."

"Let your husband do it," Amy said. "The dinner is mainly a ladies' night anyway."

"Mrs. Silvers will be there," Mrs. Anderson added.

"She's the head principal at the elementary school. If you are in good graces with her, Maria could get an early entry," Amy said.

"All my kids went there. It's an important pre-school," Mrs. Anderson said.

"We will see." Lillian nodded.

Chapter 2

Spring Cleaning

Maria, Maria!" Lillian calls. She barges into Maria's room and rips open the curtains.

Maria scrunches her eyes at the sunlight and rolls into her pillows. "What do you need, *Ma*?" she mumbles. *Ma* means mother in Khmer, a language spoken in Cambodia.

"How long are you gonna sleep, huh?"

"It's Saturday," Maria says, pulling her covers over her head.

"And?" Lillian says in a sharp tone. Amy and Mrs. Anderson warned her that kids stop listening to their parents once they turn eighteen.

"Give me a minute," Maria says.

"*La wull uy, la wull.*" Lillian shakes her head. *La wull* means lazy in Khmer. Since Lillian spoke Khmer, Tagalog, and Spanish, she had multiple ways to call Maria lazy.

Lillian drops a stack of paperwork on Maria's desk, slides a plate of freshly cut apples next to the paperwork, and leaves the room without closing the door. Maria groans loud enough so her mother can hear and then rolls out of bed. Weekends don't exist in the Lua household.

Maria picks up an apple slice and chomps on it as she runs her fingers through the documents—paperwork for her mother's work with Grow in Gaoda. Grow in Gaoda is a construction project to build new housing districts for the town. Maria's parents could not afford to pay a full-time assistant, and her father, Diego, said it was good to teach her how to work. Maria divides the stack of paperwork and fills out the accounting forms by forging her mother's signature.

When Maria was eleven, Lillian wanted Maria to attend Dalton High, Gaodan's private school. The private school required extensive applications. Maria filled out the forms with Diego, who was still practicing his written English. At that time, Lillian worked evenings while Diego worked mornings. They traded shifts often. But now that Maria was eighteen, her parents could work the same day shifts. While Lillian still worked weekends, Diego stayed home.

At eleven in the morning, Diego pops his head into Maria's room.

"You up, *mija*?" he says.

"Hi *Ba*." Maria smiles. *Ba* means father in Khmer.

Diego walks in and kisses her on the cheek. His scruffy salt-and-pepper beard tickles her cheeks and Maria scrunches her nose.

Diego laughs and ruffles Maria's hair. "You busy this weekend?" he asks.

"Well, I don't do these forms for fun."

"I can take over. You can clean the basement," Diego says.

Lillian disagreed with Diego on allowing Maria to do the extra accounting work, but Maria helped Diego learn to write in English when they filled out the forms together.

"Ma said we don't need to," Maria says.

"You're just cleaning," Diego says.

Whenever Diego brought up the idea of cleaning up the basement, Lillian would dismiss it.

"We're not selling our home," Lillian would say and hit the table because she knew it would end the discussion. Maria would not say anything when they talked about money, but she had seen their expense reports.

Maria stays silent as Diego takes the forms from her desk. He would just tell her not to worry and leave it at that.

★

Maria grabs three boxes from the storage closet and opens the basement door. She used to tell her old friends that a ghost lived behind the door so that they wouldn't open it. Her family's basement looks different compared to her friends' basements. While their basements have clean white walls, shiny floors and columns, Maria's basement has stone floors, exposed water pipes, and pink fuzz poking out of the unfinished walls.

Maria holds her breath before entering the musty room. She wears slippers because of the rough and bumpy stone staircase and floors. She holds a hand up to find the chain to the ceiling lamp. Two exposed light bulbs cast shadows on the stone walls. Their basement has low ceilings that make Diego's neck ache.

Maria shuffles to the back of the room to clear the shelves, starting from the bottom. She picks up a CD from a box of her dad's CDs of the Mexican-American guitarist Carlos Santana and the Cambodian singer Sinn Sisamouth. She sticks the disc into a CD player and hits the play button.

Maria dances to the guitar rhythms as she separates their old things into boxes to donate, sell, and keep. Diego always reminded Maria, "there's no such thing as trash." Whenever Maria accidentally ripped her clothes, her father would put them in bags to use as rags. When she broke a chair, he rebuilt it into a table and picture frame.

"Why do you keep living like we're poor?" Lillian would say to Diego.

"Because we are," Diego would want to say, but instead, he would just laugh.

Lillian stopped shopping at the Gaodan thrift stores when Mrs. Anderson saw a set of her donated plates and pillows in the Luas' home.

Maria found the thrift store four years ago when she took a hiking trail that led outside of the town. At the bottom of the hill, tucked away, is a bus stop, gas station, convenience shop, and thrift store. The thrift store had a collection of one-dollar paperbacks and three-dollar hardbacks. Maria once found a box set of urban legends around the world for only five dollars. She brought a backpack on her visits so she could fill it with discounted box sets. She opted for the adventure books.

After looking at the books, she wandered the clothing aisles. The fluffy purple sweaters or rainbow dresses would catch her eye. She would try them on but not buy them. She had a collection of black leggings and muted cardigans to wear at Dalton High. Most of the students dressed in preppy clothes or from the designer stores downtown. They would never spend a weekend at a run-down thrift store outside of town. And they would not ask where Maria found her white T-shirt and maroon cardigan. She liked it better that way.

Diego discovered Maria was going to the thrift store by her collection of used books. He suggested to Maria that she find items in their home to trade at the thrift store. Lillian insisted they needed everything they had.

Maria finds a box of her baby clothes next to the box of things to sell. Maria reminds herself to ask Diego about them and the white, folded crib tucked between the shelf and wall.

A layer of dust covers more brown boxes at the top of the shelf. Maria coughs as she pulls the boxes down to open. The last box she pulls down is full of old newspapers, pencil cases, and notebooks. At the bottom, she notices her collection of one-dollar paperback adventure books. A familiar brown leather journal hides at the bottom. Maria wipes the dust off the leather and opens the book up. Tucked inside is a stapled paper book with the title: *The Adventures of Little Lua* by Maria and Clark. On the back of the book is a short poem:

She is nurturing and kind,
absorbing the goodness in people's eyes.
But do not underestimate her might,
for Lua had quite the bite.
She followed the direction of the stars.
All around this world
are lost little girls.

"The food's going to get cold!" Lillian's voice echoes from upstairs through the floors.

"Okay!" Maria shouts.

Maria examines the paper book. Clark Chan is her uncle. She calls him *Om* Chan. *Om* means "older relative" in Khmer. She thought all of his books were lost. She hadn't heard from her uncle in ten years.

"Maria!" The light fixtures on the basement ceiling shake as Lillian stomps upstairs.

"I'm coming, *Ma*!" Maria drops the books back into the box and kicks them under the shelf.

Maria opens the door at the top of the stairs, and Lillian greets her. Her black hair is pulled into a tight ponytail, and a few strands fall around her face. She still wears her dress pants and silk white work blouse but has rolled up her sleeves.

"What are you doing down there?" Lillian crosses her arms.

"Ba asked me to…" Maria glances behind Lillian at Diego, who shakes his head. "Find his old CDs."

Maria waits for Lillian to refute, but she turns around and waves her spatula.

"I come home from a long day of work, then have to cook dinner while you just play in the basement," Lillian says. "And your father is just sitting around. Do I have to do everything?"

Maria follows Lillian into the kitchen and grabs plates to set on the table. Lillian stirs the soup and starts listing all the housework Diego could have done on his day off. Diego sits at the table, nodding, one hand pulling his beard and the other tapping his cup of café-con-leche-flavoured coffee. The smell reminds Maria of Om Chan.

When Clark visited, he would spend the mornings in the kitchen making a brew of café con leche. He would pull out the largest white mug, pour the espresso, fill it near the brim with warm milk, and mix in at least three spoons of sugar. Eight-year-old Maria watched him with wide eyes.

"That's a lot, Om," she would say.

"The sugar's the best part," Clark responded and pointed to Maria's bowl of whole-grain cereal. "Want some?"

"Ma yells at Ba when he uses lots of sugar," Maria said.

"I bet it will make it taste better." Clark held up his spoon.

Maria stirred her cereal. "She might get mad at me."

"Let her get mad at me." He sprinkled a spoon of sugar and stirred it for Maria.

She dipped her spoon in and took a bite. Clark watched her face break into a wide grin and laughs.

"I can eat it now."

"Ma doesn't need to know," Clark added.

Maria nodded and took another bite.

★

Diego catches Maria staring at his cup and slides it to her. The cup was half empty. She scrunches her nose at the strong, dark-roast scent.

"It needs sugar," Maria says. Even now, at eighteen, she snuck at least two spoons of sugar in her tea or coffee.

Diego laughs and pats the hair on the back of her head. Maria wants to ask him about Clark, but Diego always says the same thing as Lillian: "Om is busy." They have said the same answer for ten years, so Maria stopped asking.

Chapter 3

The Purple Lady

Lillian gazed at the large stage and podium at the town hall meeting. She sat at a round table covered by a white tablecloth with purple and white floral centrepieces. Other similar tables spotted the room.

The caterers maneuvered their carts of appetizers around as the townspeople filed in. The men wore dress shirts and tailored suits, while the women wore their hair in big, curly bobs paired with pearl earrings and long gloves. The women pranced around in heels and flashy cocktail dresses.

Lillian removed her hair tie, let her hair loose, and shoved her hoop earrings into her jean pocket. She wore a white button-down and faded white jeans. She sat forward so that her jeans were hidden underneath the tablecloth.

Amy and Mrs. Anderson did not mention a dress code when they urged her to join the town hall meeting for an entire month. That past weekend, when Amy and Mrs. Anderson saw Diego at the park with Maria, they visited Lillian to convince her to go to the town hall.

"You're fine. It's them who are overdressed," Mrs. Anderson assured Lillian.

Mrs. Anderson wore a long, black dress and a beaded blue necklace. Amy wore a white shirt dress and beaded earrings.

"So, this is dinner?" Lillian asked.

Mrs. Anderson and Amy nodded in unison.

"It's not too formal, but the town's catering offers free meals to new members," Amy explained.

"You get free meals for your volunteer work once you start working with the board," Mrs. Anderson added.

"Mrs. Silvers basically runs the town," Amy said.

"Her family works in all the important parts of the city," Mrs. Anderson added.

"That's her," Amy said and grabbed Lillian's arm.

Mrs. Silvers walked onto the stage and stood in front of the podium. A curly, salt-and-pepper bob framed her fair, diamond-shaped face. She wore a purple velvet dress paired with silver jewelry and pointy black heels.

"I thought you said she was a grandmother," Lillian whispered, leaning into Amy.

"She has the best aesthetician," Amy said.

"Welcome, welcome," Mrs. Silvers' low voice echoed off the walls. "What a great turnout! I see we have some new faces. I hope the weeklies don't mind if I tell my story again."

The crowd laughed.

"I know, I know. My story. Again." Mrs. Silvers paced across the stage. "I want the newcomers to feel comfortable too. You understand, right?"

The audience nodded in unison.

"First, I am glad you are all here. I am Mrs. Silvers. My daughters and granddaughters have been a part of Gaoda since the beginning…"

"Wow," Lillian said.

"She's the coolest right?" Amy said.

Lillian and Diego's coworkers mentioned the simple life outside the city and admired the post-secondary schools, daycares, and parks. Some of their kids had even worked at the warehouses. The kids saved up to attend the colleges that were a forty-five-minute bus ride out of town.

One of the coworkers' brothers had the chance to work and eventually live in Gaoda. He had said that the town's leading family helped him get an important city manager job even with his little schooling experience. Lillian and Clark were rejected from jobs outside of retail and storage facilities in Penna City because they did not finish high school.

When Lillian's grandmother Yey Chan fell sick, Lillian and Diego took a year off work to care for her. They could not afford to not work. When Yey Chan passed away, Lillian and her older brother Clark didn't expect to inherit the debt she left behind.

Diego was the reason Lillian could manage working in the warehouse each day when they were teenagers. Diego often visited her, and Clark's apartment after work. Diego and Lillian cooked dinners together. Lillian would spend most of the time talking and forget to stir the pasta on the stovetop. While she spoke, Diego would take the spoon from her and check the food.

Clark worked overtime most nights and joined them at six thirty in the evening when dinner was ready. Diego always made him an extra plate and asked him to join.

"Why do you kiss up to my brother so much?" Lillian teased Diego one night.

"He could be my brother." Diego smirked.

Lillian smacked Diego's hand and laughed. Diego put Lillian at ease with her brother by talking to Clark when he was moody. Ever since Yey Chan died, Clark took over their grandmother's constant nagging, especially when she would talk about how Lillian and Diego spent their time and money.

One week when Diego was sick, Lillian had dinners alone with Clark. They didn't have anything to talk about other than work.

"I don't want to pack boxes for the rest of my life," Lillian said.

"Be grateful for a job, *oun*." Clark said. *Oun* refers to a younger person in Khmer.

"All the other women just gossip all day. I wish we would talk about better things."

"Like what?" Clark leaned forward.

"Anything else besides their kids, their sister's kids, and their brother's kids."

"Can't a person brag about their kids?"

"Why are you defending them?"

"I'm just saying."

"Why can't you let me complain?" Lillian slapped her knee, although she wanted to slap Clark's arm.

"It is not good for you," Clark said.

Lillian shrunk in her chair.

"You're getting paid well. I should be the one complaining," Clark continued.

"Then take my job." Lillian crossed her arms.

"You are lucky to work. You're just going to throw it away?"

★

Clark would probably scold Lillian now for not engaging with the other women around the table with her. Lillian looked at Amy and Mrs. Anderson sitting on either side of her. Lillian stared at the centerpiece of purple and white flowers. She heard bits of the other women's conversations. They reminded her of the women at the warehouse, who talked about their kids' university plans.

"Mrs. Lua," a husky voice said behind Lillian.

"Yes?" Lillian turned to a short man in a grey suit. He hugged a clipboard, and lanyards hung off his wrist.

"Mrs. Silvers requested to meet you in private," he said.

"Really?" Amy and Mrs. Anderson said at the same time.

"Please follow me," the man said.

Lillian followed the man in the grey suit through a long, red-carpeted hallway. The wooden, dark brown walls were adorned with gold scones and tall portrait paintings of men in suits and women in dresses. They stopped at the end of the hall, and the man opened two doors that led into a large office.

The grey floral wallpaper looked lilac under the warm glow of the silver lamps against the wall. Mrs. Silvers sat in an oversized leather chair behind a shiny, grey desk with a teacup in her hand. Behind her hung a gallery of maps and photos of homes with laughing families.

"Hi Lillian. Please make yourself at home," Mrs. Silvers said. She smiled and held out her hand, pointing towards the grey, cotton sofa across from her.

"Nice to meet you, Miss." Lillian bowed and sat down. Her eyes wandered the room. She glimpsed at some of the items on Mrs. Silver's desk: a glass clock, a cup with silver and gold pens, and a leather purple notebook.

"I wanted to thank you for coming to our meeting and personally introduce myself. I love seeing our town grow." Mrs. Silvers grinned.

"A very nice place," Lillian said. She played with the threads of the holes in her jeans.

"Great for young couples. We are here to help everyone, okay?"

Lillian nodded.

"You moved from the inner city, right?" Mrs. Silvers looked Lillian up and down.

Amy had explained before that Mrs. Silvers was well-connected. She knew everything about everyone, from education to professional experience. Amy said it was part of the screening process for accepting new Gaodans into town.

"Yes, I'm from Penna City." Lillian let go of her jeans and folded her hands.

Most of the neighbours didn't know what Penna City was until Diego and Lillian told them they lived near the inner city. Penna City is a multicultural district with lots of tiny homes and apartments. Factories and warehouses lined the streets. It was less than a two-hour drive from Gaoda.

"Have you found work?" Mrs. Silvers leaned forward.

"Not yet."

"Well, lucky for you, I have an upcoming project I need help with." Mrs. Silvers slid a booklet across the table. "Have you heard of Grow in Gaoda?"

A photo of a smiling family of four covered the face of the booklet. Lillian flipped through the book of maps, blueprints, and house layouts inside. Mrs. Silvers explained that their expansion project needed assistance with management and construction. She heard that Lillian was bilingual and noted many immigrant workers were involved in their project. Mrs. Silvers also offered a position to Diego to help with the construction work.

"It's not glamourous, I know, but it's work we need," Mrs. Silvers said.

"I don't have much experience with translating," Lillian said, twiddling her thumbs.

Lillian learned to speak Khmer and Tagalog from Yey Chan and picked up Spanish from Diego, their coworkers and past neighbours. She could hold a basic conversation in Spanish because there were many common words with Tagalog.

"What matters is that you can have a conversation in both languages." Mrs. Silvers rested her elbows on the desk and held her hands at her lips. "You can also learn."

"Why me?" Lillian said.

"It must be difficult to move your life. We're a giving town and want to lend a hand to young people like you." Mrs. Silvers tilted her head. "Some of our workers are from the inner city, too. It might be nice for them to see a friendly face."

"I will have to talk to my husband," Lillian said, holding the booklet to her chest.

Maria was barely a one-year-old, and Diego just started working at a warehouse again. But Lillian thought about how it would be good for the both of them to work in Gaoda and see each other on weekdays.

"Think about it," Mrs. Silvers said.

Chapter 4

Sol and Lua

Maria sat on her bed and clutched Clark's journals to her chest. She learned to wrap her arms around herself when she felt like sinking into her worries. What happened to her Om ten years ago? Her memories of Clark flooded back after she cleaned the basement last week and found his old journals and stories.

When Maria was six years old, Clark babysat her for two months while Lillian and Diego went to a work conference. The first week her parents were away, Maria cried every night, and Clark sat in her room until she fell asleep. Clark read aloud Diego's book of fairy tales, but he couldn't do the same voices Diego did.

One night, Clark suggested they make their own story. He opened his brown leather journal and grabbed a pen. "It needs a cool character," he said.

"Like you?" Maria said.

"Ah, Om's too old for adventures," he laughed and shook his head. "How about you? We'll call her Lua."

"Okay." Maria moved closer to peak into Clark's notebook.

"We don't want her to be alone…" Clark said. "Does she have a sidekick?"

"What about a big tiger?" she widened her arms.

He tickles Maria. "A tiger for Lua to fight?"

"No, it's a nice one."

"You don't think tiger's are scary?" Clark bit off his pen cap.

"No, he is nice and helps Lua travel," Maria said.

"Huh. A big friendly tiger…" Clark scribbled in his journal. "I like it."

"He looks like that." Maria pointed at the tattoo on his arm. Wrapped around his bicep is a Bengal tiger, drawn with wavy black stripes. The tiger looks off to the distance, and its head looks fluffy with long whiskers.

"So, what's the tiger's name?" Clark asked.

"Roar!" Maria jumped onto Clark.

Clark lifted her up and tickled her. That night, Maria slept without crying.

The next night, they planned to make a series. Clark wrote down all of their ideas and revealed his sketches to Maria.

The main character of the book, Lua, had long, black hair and wore white boxy dresses. In the first book, Lua travels with her tiger companion, Sol, to find her parents. Sol and Lua were the same height.

"What happened to them?" Maria touched the drawing.

"They are lost," Clark said.

"Why aren't parents in fairy tales?" Maria looked up.

"They would stop the adventure," Clark said and flipped to the next page.

★

When Maria's parents came home, she and Clark did not touch their story again. Clark went back to work in Penna City. He visited some weekends but did not stay overnight.

When Maria was eight years old, Lillian and Diego worked the same shifts through the weekends, so

Clark came back and stayed over to watch Maria from Thursday to Sunday nights.

One day, after school, Maria and Clark sat at the kitchen table that was covered in books and lined paper. Clark had a writing assignment for his freelance travel writing job, but struggled to find a story without travelling. Maria had a homework assignment to draw and write a short story. Maria stared at the blank page, kicking her feet under the table. She needed to present her story to her class. In her last story presentation, her friend Remy Anderson joked that the character she drew looked nothing like Maria.

Remy and her mother, Mrs. Anderson, used to visit Maria and Lillian often. Remy was taller and loved to hold items over Maria's head and watch Maria struggle on her tiptoes. Remy always pointed out how Maria looked or what she wore when she noticed Maria wearing their friend Farren's old clothes. Maria was shorter than Farren, so most of Farren's shirts almost fell past her knees, and her pants would billow at Maria's ankles.

"How can you wear someone else's clothes?" Remy asked one day in math class, crossing her arms. She tilted her head, and her blond ponytail swung back and forth. Remy turned to Farren. "Why did you give them to her?"

"I like them," Maria said before Farren could answer. Maria looked down at the rolled-up sleeves of her sweater. The fabric bunched up at her shoulders. It felt comfortable to hide in soft, thick layers. She tugged at her jeans. Diego sewed their hems, but the jeans were still loose around her waist, and she needed to wear them with a belt.

"My mom gave them to her," Farren admitted, playing with a strand of her strawberry blonde hair.

"You're swimming in them," Remy laughed, pulling at the bottom of the sweater. "Looks like someone wants to be Farren."

After school, Maria went home and stuffed Farren's clothes into a box and dumped them on the side of the road. Lillian yelled at Maria when she found out. She walked into the house and dropped the box in front of Maria. "Why are you throwing this away?" she said.

"I don't want them," Maria replied. "They're not my own clothes."

"*Jung ramo gon?*" Do you want to be ungrateful? Lillian said in Khmer.

Maria shook her head and took the box back inside. When Lillian went to work, Maria hid the box in the basement.

Maria thought it was just the clothes Remy didn't like. But Remy also commented on how tiny Maria looked and sometimes pretended not to see her at school.

In Maria's last drawing, she drew herself as a princess with pencil crayons. She used the colour peach for the skin, light brown for her face and hair, and drew on a purple dress and a flower crown. Remy, Farren, and Maria sat around the table together, waiting to present their drawings.

Remy peered over Maria's shoulder to look at her drawing and said, "that looks nothing like you."

"I just made her up," Maria said.

Remy grabbed the page and said, "it looks more like Farren."

"It's a pretty drawing," Farren said.

"A princess? Are you four?" Remy laughed. "That's so childish."

That evening, Maria sat at the table, twirling her pencil.

"Need help?" Clark said. "We can help each other out."

Maria told Clark that her friends didn't like her stories. Clark searched through piles of paper and books on the table and pulled out his brown leather journal.

"We wrote some good stories before," Clark said. He opened the journal and slid Maria a copy of one of their books.

"They're too silly," Maria said. "It needs to be cool."

"Fairy tale adventures aren't cool anymore?" Clark tilted his head.

Maria shook her head. She decided to write a story about a grown-up girl in school playing with her friends. On another paper, Maria doodled the characters she made with Clark—a tiny bright-eyed girl and her kind and wise tiger.

Maria saved the drawings to show them to Clark the next weekend, but he didn't show up that week. Or the next. She knew he sometimes snuck in late Friday nights when she heard the front door slam, but the house was quiet.

Maria waited until her parents fell asleep. She closed her eyes, held her blanket at her chin, and listened for

Lillian. When she heard her Diego's loud snores, she rolled out of bed and snuck outside to check the living room in case Clark came home. The pile of blankets on the couch was still folded. The coffee table was clean of his stacks of journals and empty coffee mugs.

Lillian woke up and yelled at Maria to go back to bed. Instead, Maria crawled into Lillian and Diego's bed and lay down between them.

"Where's *Om*?" Maria pulled on the sleeve of Lillian's nightgown.

"He went back home for a while," Lillian said.

"Why?" Maria said.

"He's just busy," Lillian replied and pressed her forehead to Maria's.

"Did I do something?" Maria whispered.

"What could you do, *mija*?" Diego patted her hair.

★

Maria sits up in her bed and opens the front cover of Clark's journal. Inside, she finds the first story they wrote and stapled together: *The Adventures of Little Lua* by Maria and Clark. Maria had used a star-shaped hole puncher for the construction-paper cover and cut out a girl and a tiger. She opens the book. Inscribed on the first page in messy, cursive red ink is a note that says:

To my light, you're the reason I write. The reason I open my eyes to watch you gaze at the stars and reach for the moon. No dream is too small. It is yours, all yours.

Maria turned the page and read the story.

Lua stared out towards the castle. One day, she will be back in the safe stone walls. But for now, she is a hopeless, lost light. Half a flower sits in her hand. She holds it tight and worries it will take days to travel.

In her sleep, she called out, "Please, I am alone. I need a guide."

When she awoke, she met a tiger's eyes. She steps back, ready to fight. It circles around her. She notices it's gaze— fierce and faithful. She holds out a hand, and the tiger jumps forward. It leans its head into her hands and nudges her. She climbs on and hugs the tiger. It jumps up over high bushes.

"What should I call you?" Lua laughs.

As the tiger jumps, Lua feels its warmth below her. The tiger's bright orange fur glows under the sun.

She leans down into its soft fur and whispers, "I'll call you Sol."

Chapter 5

The Man with the Tiger Tattoo

I thought you'd visit me," Clark said once Diego opened the front door. Clark lived in Penna, a city that was a two-hour drive from Gaoda.

"*Bong!*" Diego extended a hand to his brother-in-law, then yanked him into a hug. *Bong* refers to an older person in Khmer.

"Are you ignoring me?" Clark laughed.

"We meant to visit you in Penna last month, but I have been working a lot."

"I see." Clark looked Diego up and down.

Diego's messy, curly black hair grew out past his jaw, and his chin had a hint of stubble. Diego wore a grey, oversized, stained t-shirt and plaid pajama pants.

"It's my day off," Diego laughed. "Sorry, I don't look as good as you."

"Thanks, brother." Clark flashed a smile. His broad shoulders made him look big in the narrow doorway, and he wore a black tank top that exposed the tattoos dancing up his right arm to the back of his neck. They consisted of diagonal lines, lotus flowers, and a tiger on his right bicep. A bulky black duffel bag sat at his feet. "Where is Lil?" Clark poked his head in the doorway.

"She was sleeping." Diego stepped back and ushered Clark in.

Diego showed off their small living room and attached kitchen. Clark smiled at his photos of Penna City on their wall. They were pictures of strangers waiting for buses and plants on empty windows.

Diego and Clark sat at the kitchen table. They caught up on sports, work, and Lillian's no-sleep lifestyle until a small, whiny noise escaped the baby monitor next to them.

"Finally." Clark stood up and clapped his hands.

"I thought you came to see me," Diego joked.

He led Clark down the hallway into Maria's dim nursery, lit up by the paper lanterns she could not sleep without. Lillian stood over the crib, adjusting Maria's blankets.

"Someone's finally up." Clark walked up and placed a hand on Lillian's back.

She jumped, then turned and slapped his arm.

"Hey, when did you get here?" Lillian said.

"Nice to see you too." Clark smirked.

She hit his arm again then pulled him into a hug.

Clark pulled away, then pushed her aside and walked up to Maria. "Now, what I am actually here for." He peered over the crib.

An eight-month-old Maria stared back at him. She was wrapped up tight in a white blanket, so only her face was visible. Her mouth twitched up slightly, and her eyes looked wide and glossy. Lillian observed them, ready to grab Maria in case she cried.

Clark turned to Lillian. "May I?"

Lillian nodded.

Clark lifted Maria up and cradled the back of her head carefully. Maria was almost half the size of his muscles. He leaned down and whispered in her ear. Then looked back up and flashed a smile at Lillian and Diego.

"Maria likes you." Diego smiled.

"What did you say to her?" Lillian crossed her arms.

"It's between us." Clark held Maria up into his chest.

"She's my daughter," Lillian said.

"She is." Clark leaned forward to ruffle the top of Lillian's head. "I am happy for you."

Lillian's frown softened into a smile. "Thank you, Bong."

Clark planned to stay the night then head back to work on Sunday. He made a pit stop at Lillian and Diego's because his next photography assignment was a three-hour drive away from Gaoda.

Lillian and Diego suggested making dinner that night the way they used to in Clark's apartment in the city when Lillian and Diego were newlyweds. Clark sat at the kitchen table talking about his work while Lillian chopped peppers. Diego hunched over the stove, stir-frying rice and beef.

"So, enough about me," Clark finally said when they brought the finished stir-fried rice to the table. "How's suburbia?"

"Some adjusting," Diego said.

"You're working, right?" Clark said.

"There's a job I am looking at," Lillian said. "It's for a city expansion project. I would translate and guide the workers."

Lillian glanced at Diego. She briefly mentioned her conversation with Mrs. Silvers to him, but they only talked about it a little bit.

"Wait, where are they building this?" Clark said.

"The Shae district," Lillian said. "It's near Penna."

The Shae district was like the inner city, but it was smaller. It was a town that was full of run-down motels and apartments. Many of Lillian and Diego's old coworkers from Penna lived in Shae because it only took twenty minutes to ride a bus to work.

"Hmm, why does that sound familiar?" Clark said, poking at the peppers on his plate with his fork.

They all sat in silence for a moment.

"Should I do it? Even if I am not qualified?" Lillian asked them.

"Nonsense," Diego said. "You'd do a great job."

She looked at Clark.

"Does it pay well?" he asked.

On Sunday evening, Amy took Lillian to the next town hall dinner. Lillian wore her nicest black dress and straightened her naturally wavy hair. Mrs. Anderson joined them at the table but sat across from them.

As they waited, Amy grabbed Lillian's arm and whispered, "I heard Diego is talking to some weird strangers."

"What?" Lillian said.

"Last weekend, he was with some guy…who was definitely not from Gaoda," Amy said. "He was carrying around some black bag."

"Oh…Clark?"

"Do you know him?"

"Yeah, he's my—"

"Hello, hello," Mrs. Silvers deep voice boomed.

Speakers lined each corner of the room to ensure everyone could hear her. She stood in the centre of the stage, scanning each face as she tapped her heel. She looked at each table, waiting until they turned to look at her.

"Now, let's start." Mrs. Silvers folded her hands.

During the town hall meeting, the townspeople covered fundraising events at the schools and volunteer initiatives to help the students. They wanted to prep the town's students for university and college, which meant helping them build strong portfolios starting in middle school.

Lillian watched how Mrs. Silvers moved across the stage. Under the soft stage lights, her long, lilac, silk dress shone. Lillian froze when Mrs. Silvers' sharp blue eyes met hers.

Mrs. Silvers extended her hand towards Lillian. "I'd like to introduce a new face to Gaoda. Lillian Lua. She's representing a new line of young families and has stepped up to help the town's expansion projects. Thank you for joining us, Lillian."

Lillian rises from her chair and bows to the crowd's cheers.

"You're working for Mrs. Silvers?" Mrs. Anderson asked Lillian once the applause died down.

Lillian nodded.

"How did you manage that?" Mrs. Anderson said.

"She told me she wanted to help out new families," Lillian said.

"Huh."

"Yeah."

Mrs. Anderson sat back and turned her head towards the stage. She and Lillian didn't talk for the rest of the night. Later that evening, Lillian waited for

Diego outside. She sat in a garden area that separated a pathway with tall hedges. Behind them, she heard Mrs. Anderson and another woman's voice.

"She's not even from Gaoda," Mrs. Anderson said. "Why would Mrs. Silvers work with her?"

Lillian leaned back, feeling the leaves of the hedge poke through the back of her dress.

"Don't you sit at that girl's table?" the other woman said.

"I could run an expansion project. I run all the high school projects," Mrs. Anderson continued. Her heels clicked against the pavement.

"They said they wanted new kinds of families," the other woman continued.

"Yeah, they're definitely a different kind of family," Mrs. Anderson said. Her voice and heel clicks softened. "Did you hear about that tattooed man at their house?"

Chapter 6

Silvers' Secrets

Lillian studied how to translate language during her maternity leave. While watching Maria, Lillian would put on a telenovela in Spanish, or a Korean drama dubbed in Khmer or Tagalog. Lillian also translated Maria's fairy tale books by writing them out in Khmer and Tagalog. When she finished those, she translated Yey Chan's book of ghost stories. Maria would stare at the pages of the books while sucking on her finger. Lillian had to stop reading them when Diego heard Maria say *kamoych*, meaning "ghost" in Khmer.

Lillian joined Mrs. Silvers' expansion project when Maria turned two years old. She was surprised at how simple some of her tasks were on her first day. She translated morning meetings then wrote them out for their records. But since she joined the project late and had a lot of catching up to do, Lillian worked late into the evening when Diego had to work at the warehouse.

Mrs. Silvers offered to help take care of Maria on the nights she was watching her own two-year-old granddaughter, Farren. One night, when Mrs. Silvers was babysitting Farren, and Lillian and Diego weren't working late, she invited them for dinner. The moment Farren saw Maria, she crawled up to her and handed her a toy. Lillian smiled because Maria did not cry.

After work one evening, Lillian joined Mrs. Silvers on Mrs. Silvers' back porch. They watched Maria and Farren play in the backyard. The two toddlers sat on a picnic blanket, ripped out grass and pebbles, then threw them into plastic bowls to serve to a line of Farren's large stuffed animals.

"I hope they can be good friends," Lillian said. "Maria is a shy one."

"They can be good for each other," Mrs. Silvers said, watching Farren jump up and tackle her fluffy, stuffed tiger while Maria continued to fill the plastic bowls with grass.

"I think so." Lillian smiled.

"You have to watch who your daughter plays with," Mrs. Silvers said. "Good influences only."

"Is that something I can even control?" Lillian said.

"Of course. It starts young. You decide who your kids can play with and who takes care of them," Mrs. Silvers explained.

"That's true."

Lillian watched Maria serve the bowls to the stuffed animals' plates while Farren ran around collecting sticks. Lillian reminded Maria every time they came over to play nice and calm around Mrs. Silvers. "Only good girls can play at Mrs. Silvers' home, okay?" Lillian would say.

Maria always had to play nice around Farren, even when Farren was hyperactive. They stuck together during middle school and walked home together every day until Farren started to play soccer in grade six. Farren suggested Maria join the team too, but Maria wasn't competitive. Farren's teammates yelled at Maria in gym class for not catching the ball when she was the goalie or not kicking it far enough down the field. They laughed at her when her voice cracked.

"Are you going to cry?" Remy teased.

"I just want to play for fun," Maria would say.

Maria preferred to read or draw in the quiet classrooms during recess anyways.

On Tuesdays and Thursdays, Farren joined Maria's walks home. Farren learned a lot from girls' locker rooms after soccer practice because they were in grades seven and eight. The grade-eight girls knew a lot about their neighbourhood. They knew enough that when Farren walked down her street, she could point out a house and reveal a secret about the family that lived there.

Farren told Maria that her next-door neighbours kept their daughter away from school because she is sixteen and pregnant with twins. She told Maria the daughter wanted to keep her babies, but the parents didn't like the boyfriend.

Farren also gossiped about how her other next-door neighbours had three reckless sons. One son was in rehab for substance abuse and the other two attended a military boarding school. Maria remembered that when she first saw those neighbours, they liked to chase their golden retriever around with muddy hands. The youngest brother would stack up dirt to form a little muddy hill. Mrs. Silvers would not let Maria and Farren play with the boys. She said they were too messy.

One day after Farren's soccer game, Maria and Farren took a different route that passed Maria's house first. When they reached Maria's street, Farren said, "Most of these families are broke. Remy said they're all temporary houses for people who stay for a year then leave."

Maria paused in her steps.

"Are you okay?" Farren stopped.

"I thought I dropped something." Maria studied the ground.

"We shouldn't stay in this part of the neighbour-hood too long." Farren hooked her arm with Marias.

"Right," Maria said.

Farren only visited Maria's house once, so she must have forgotten where Maria lived. Their school was near the middle of the city, about six minutes away from the Silvers home. Once Farren got home, Maria walked another fifteen minutes to reach her own house.

As they walked down Maria's street, Farren pointed at a few townhouses. When they arrived at Maria's corner house, Farren looked at it and said, "apparently, that's a sketchy house. Remy said they have a drug dealer that goes by there a lot."

Maria, still hooked to Farren, kept walking so Farren wouldn't get suspicious again. She felt relieved when Farren didn't notice that Maria was quieter than usual. Maria didn't talk much anyway.

When Maria said goodbye to Farren, she noticed how big Farren's house was. It had a long deck, wide porch stairs, and columns. A black fence lined her lawn that had three large trees. Maria counted the trees on each lawn as she walked pass each street. The number of trees on each lawn went from three to one by the time she reached the townhouses.

Maria's house had one floor unless you counted the basement. The kitchen and living room weren't separated rooms like Farren's house.

Lillian stood in the kitchen with plastic lunch containers laid out around her. She raised an eyebrow at Maria, who stood in the doorway looking around the house.

"You're late," Lillian said.

"Farren had a soccer game tonight," Maria said, walking towards the hallway.

"I see," Lillian said, "did you eat yet?"

"I will eat later," Maria said.

Maria walked into her bedroom, dropped her bag onto the floor and jumped into a pile of pillows on her bed. She didn't question why her parents worked longer hours or barely saw each other. She thought all parents did that. But the bleachers at Farren's soccer games were always full of families sipping on slushies and munching on popcorn.

Maria didn't get allowances, so she would sit on the furthest end of the bleachers near the fence with a water bottle and sketchbook. She looked up every now and then in case Farren was looking at the bleachers, but Farren was always focused on the game. She was always wrapped up in something, which is why Maria thought she talked a lot. Farren just wanted to let everyone know about everything she did.

"You okay, *mija?*" Diego asked. He stood at the doorway of her bedroom, wearing his warehouse polo shirt. His curly hair looked flattened from his safety hat.

"Just tired."

Diego walked in and kissed Maria on the forehead. His clothes smelled like propane from the warehouse forklifts. "Don't study too hard."

"How was work?" Maria asked him. She sat up and re-fluffed the pillow she collapsed on.

"Ah, you know…" Diego paused and patted Maria's hair. "I'm happy at home."

Maria smiled. She didn't know what else to say or ask.

"You had a soccer game?" Diego asked.

"It was Farren's game."

"Oh," Diego said. He turned around and walked toward the door. "Dinner at seven, okay?" he said as he walked out.

Diego wanted Maria to spend less time with Farren and the Silvers, but Lillian kept calling Mrs. Silvers and asking about her granddaughter. Diego noticed how active and talkative Farren was. At only seven years old, she would talk non-stop about other kids and families in the town. They were things a little kid shouldn't know. Diego told Farren to be careful of what she said.

The next time Lillian and Diego picked Maria up from Mrs. Silvers' house, Mrs. Silvers told Diego in a sharp tone, "watch your own kid, not mine."

"She fills mine with bad ideas," Diego replied, enunciating every word so that his Spanish accent wouldn't slip out.

"My granddaughter keeps Maria out of trouble," Mrs. Silvers snapped. "Do you want her to stop?"

"Mrs. Silvers, I think this is just a little misunderstanding." Lillian stepped in.

"Farren says your husband's calling her a liar." Mrs. Silvers crossed her arms.

"I tell her no lying to Maria," Diego corrected.

Lillian snapped back at Diego in Spanish, "You can't say that to someone's kid."

"She misunderstands. I don't want our daughter to become a liar like her granddaughter," he replied in Spanish.

"That's worse," Lillian said in Spanish.

Mrs. Silvers taps her foot impatiently.

"Just apologize," Lillian said.

"I don't want problems." Diego looked at Mrs. Silvers. "I am sorry."

Mrs. Silvers clicked her tongue but nodded for Diego to leave. As he walked down the porch steps, she grabbed Lillian's arm as she stepped down. Lillian looked up at the old lady. "Does he understand?"

"Of course."

"He has no right to say anything to my girl."

Lillian nodded and then bowed. "It won't happen again."

"We have to be on Mrs. Silver's good side," Lillian said to Diego at home. "She watches our kid."

"I know," Diego said. But he couldn't shake his annoyance with the Silvers. He didn't want them to know about his home life, especially since they were a family of gossips. He didn't want Maria to get hurt either.

Diego noticed Maria's fondness for the Silvers siblings. She often talked about Farren's sisters and about wanting her own sisters.

"Or brothers—because I'm not picky," Maria would say after spending a day with the Silvers.

Diego would remind Lillian that they couldn't afford another kid. But that excuse sounded better than their reality. With the other parents around them announcing their third and fourth children, Lillian would talk to Diego about having another child for Maria's sake. Lillian said she wanted Maria to have a reliable friend after seeing her play so well with Farren. They started trying after Maria turned two.

Getting pregnant did not happen as easily as the first time. Lillian told Mrs. Silvers about their complications, and Mrs. Silvers recommended some of the best midwives. They offered expensive treatments to help, but they didn't guarantee fertility.

"We help you with what you can control," the doctors had said.

It took Lillian and Diego their second missed mortgage payment to realize they couldn't keep trying. After countless doctor appointments with OB/GYNs and midwives, Diego and Lillian could not get pregnant again.

"Maybe we're just unlucky," Lillian said as she stared out the car window on their way home from an appointment at the fertility clinic.

"The doctor said it's very common," Diego assured her. "They said it was most likely secondary infertility."

"I know," Lillian sighed.

Diego's eyes stayed on the road. He thought about Mrs. Silvers' next expensive suggestion and shook his head. "Why did we have to tell her?" he said.

Lillian wrapped her arms up to her chest and stared out the car window.

Chapter 7

A Cup of Café con Leche

Maria searches through Google for Clark Chan in between classes. Her parents don't talk much about their life before Gaoda, but she knows they lived in another city just before she was born.

Maria's parents did not graduate high school, but Diego once mentioned Penna City and Shae College a few hours away from Gaoda. Maria types in the school's names and finds an old article written by someone named Clark Chan. She bookmarked the page. In the distance, she overhears the other seniors talk about choosing their colleges during their week off for March break.

It takes Maria the next two weeks to plan a trip to Penna City to find her uncle. She trades her old clothes and books at the thrift store for cash credit. Now, she just has to convince her parents.

On Sunday morning, Maria joins Lillian and Diego at the table with college guidebooks from the student council office.

"March break is coming up, and they are doing college tours," Maria says, spreading out the booklets. "I was wondering if I can go to them?"

"I don't know if we have time to take you right now," Diego says, tapping on his empty coffee mug and glancing at the stove where his kettle boils.

"Why can't you go to school here?" Lillian says, studying the college booklets. "Isn't Gaodan College a top school?"

"What if I don't get in?" Maria says, "I need a backup. Everyone has one. Even Farren."

"You've never stayed out of town like this. On your own." Lillian crosses her arms.

"I won't be alone," Maria lies. "Some of my class-mates are going."

"This doesn't look cheap." Lillian picks up the booklet.

"I am sure we can help her pay for the trip," Diego grabs the booklet from Lillian and flips through.

"Diego," Lillian snaps.

"She's old enough," Diego says. "It's good for her to look at her college options."

"I will be careful," Maria adds.

Lillian glares at Diego.

Diego flips to the pages with the tuition breakdown and slides it to Lillian. "Think ahead," he says.

She sighs and turns to Maria. "You must call me in the morning, afternoon, and evening."

★

Maria clutches her duffel bag throughout the bus ride and stares out the window. They pass lush trees and large homes. As they move further from Gaoda, Maria notices more factories, motels, and apartment complexes.

The bus reaches Penna City Station Terminal in two hours. Once Maria gets off the bus, she pulls out her phone map to the last saved address. The map marks an apartment complex just a two-minute walk away.

There are no sidewalks, so Maria walks on the side of the street, maneuvering the parked cars. She stops outside a small apartment complex at the end of the road. She walks in and adjusts her sweater because the building is warm and smells like skunk and Febreze.

Maria turns to the list of residents and runs her hand to the top, searching for the letter C: *C. Chan: Room 403.*

Her finger lingers on the call button. Maria spent the day rehearsing what to say and do, and now she is here.

A loud beep startles Maria. She turns to see a resident holding the door open for her. She rushes in, hugging her duffel bag. Inside it, she packed clothes, schoolwork, and Clark's journals.

Maria takes the elevator to the fourth floor. On her right, at the end of the hall, is Room 403. There is no peephole on the door. She knocks. No answer. Maria rocks back and forth on her heels, glancing back at the elevator. She knocks once more. Then, the door creaks open. Clark squints at her, and wrinkles form on his forehead.

"Hi Om," Maria says, adjusting the strap of her bag that digs into her right shoulder.

He opens the door wider and pulls up the glasses that hang on a chain around his neck. "Maria?"

"Yes."

Clark smiles. Like an instinct, his hand reaches for the top of her head, but he pulls back. Instead, he pushes the door open, steps back, and says, "Come in."

He led Maria to an old leather couch in the middle of the room. Maria looks around at the brick walls decorated with photos and the countertop and coffee tables covered in papers, photographs, and empty take-out containers.

"Coffee?" Clark asks, walking to the kitchen counter behind the couch.

"I prefer tea—if you have it," Maria says.

Clark walks over and places two large white mugs, a pot of sugar, and one spoon down on an empty spot on the table. Maria leans forward and scrunches her nose at the dark roast aroma from Clark's cup.

"Too strong?" Clark laughs.

Maria nods. "I find coffee bitter. Even with sugar."

"Wow, if I had your dad to make me coffee, I'd drink it all the time." Clark mixes in two spoons of sugar into his café-con-leche-flavoured coffee.

Maria takes his spoon and adds two sugars to the tea. Clark smiles at her, and they sip their drinks together. He studies how his niece's face has changed.

Maria had a full face that slimmed down to reveal high cheekbones like Lillian's.

"How's your Ma?" Clark says.

"Good, she works a lot," Maria says.

"Not surprised." Clark nods.

Maria nods back. They sip their drinks in silence. The heat of the coffee slightly fogs up Clark's glasses that slide down his nose. When Clark catches Maria staring at him, she averts her eyes down then leans forward to examine the coffee table.

"Have you been writing?" Maria says.

"Not much. These are old projects," Clark says, staring at the piles of his old work.

"I see."

"So, what brings you here?"

"It's March break." Maria pulls on the bottom of her sweater. "So, I am looking at colleges in Penna."

"College already?" Clark picks at the leather pieces falling off the couch.

"Yes," Maria says. "I turn nineteen soon."

"Wow," Clark says. "And your parents let you come to the city?"

"They know I'm looking at colleges."

"Where are you staying?"

"A motel near South Inca, I think."

"Oh, that's not a good place," Clark says, looking back up at Maria. "You should stay here."

That evening, Clark sleeps on the couch and gives Maria his bed. The apartment is warm at night, so Clark leaves the windows open and gives her extra blankets. In bed, Maria listens to the conversations of passing strangers. Their voices help her fall asleep because they kept her from swimming in her own thoughts. Especially because she has a lot of questions for Clark.

The following day, Clark tells Maria he needs to work and apologizes because he can't spend time with her. Maria tells him she has schoolwork to keep her busy. He cleans up the kitchen table for her to study.

While studying, Maria glances at his shelf of journals. She wonders if Clark remembers *The Adventures of Little Lua*, since he left his brown leather journal at her house many years ago. She takes out the little book from her bag and doodles scenes from their stories. In the afternoon, she goes into his bedroom to lie down.

It's dark when Maria wakes up. She walks into the kitchen and finds Clark standing behind the counter.

"Morning," he jokes, then slides a box of cupcakes towards her. "You still like sweets?"

"Of course." Maria smiles, hops onto a seat, and opens the box.

"I didn't know where those stories went," Clark says, pointing at the purple book Maria left on the counter.

"You still remember those?" Maria says.

"Of course." Clark walks towards his shelf, grabs a thick journal, and places it in front of Maria. "I've written a few other things inspired by Lua."

Maria takes the journal, and flips through Clark's writing.

Fae's Dealings

Fae shares every detail,
Every thought, from every friend.
Every promise, you defend.
Fae hears your secrets and your sins,
They know stories from within.
Be careful of what you say,
Fae will find it and give it away.
Little Lua, hold on,
A Fae's dealings are never wrong.

The Moon Knights

The Moon Knights look noble and kind,
Under the light, their armor glimmers and shines.
No one notices their faces below,
Well-guarded are eyes aglow,
They look yellow and sour,
Ugly with selfishness and power.
Get me their helmet, Little Lua, and you will see.
The Moon Knights are not who they appear to be.

Lady Lilac

Don't be fooled by her lilac locks,
The pink flowers twisted in her hair.
She smells sweet,
Her words tempting.
She leads you to your personal home.
"It's what you want."
You walk in, and the ice settles over,
Her hair turns silver.
You reach out to her,
But her hand is cold,
Her eyes confining.
Sol is gone.
Lua cradles herself, cries.
Everything she ever felt,
Dismissed with her Silver eyes.

Chapter 8

Grow in Gaoda

At a town event one weekend, Lillian searched the crowd for a sight of Mrs. Silvers' purple accessories like her burgundy neck scarf or lavender designer bag. Lillian found Mrs. Silvers alone at the corner table with her burgundy neck scarf wrapped around her neck. Lillian slid into the seat next to her.

They made small talk about how Maria went up a reading level in school and how Mrs. Silvers' grand-daughter Farren joined the soccer team. Then, Mrs. Silvers asked Lillian for a progress update with the Gaodan expansion project.

"We are losing some workers next month," Lillian said.

"Yeah, the investors won't be happy," Mrs. Silvers said, tapping her long, burgundy-coloured fingernails on the desk.

Even though Lillian was just the messenger between the workers and management, she felt a tug of guilt in her stomach when she told management a worker was leaving the project. Since she had to translate the conversations, Lillian sat with the workers and helped them go through their resignation and departure forms and explained the agreements.

Lillian would tap the red pen on the desk and ask the last question. "Why are you leaving?"

"*Extraño a mi familia*," one of the construction workers, Amelia had said in Spanish. She spoke on how she missed her family. The work included extensive hours, long travel time and hard labour.

Lillian wrote down "personal reasons."

A few weeks later, Carlos sat in the office with Lillian to request resignation.

"*Ellos estan locos*," They are crazy, Carlos said in Spanish.

Lillian wrote, "different atmosphere and unexpected management changes."

"I don't like Gaoda," *Kuya* Roman had said. He was a kind and honest older Filipino man who told Lillian to refer to him as *Kuya*, meaning "uncle" in Tagalog. Kuya Roman spoke English well but did not know how to read or write.

Lillian tapped the red pen to her lip and said, "I don't know if I can write that."

"That's my reason. Why can't you write that?" Kuya Roman peered at the forms.

Lillian filtered the workers' answers and avoided saying anything negative about Gaoda. On the first resignation request she filled out with an older Khmer man, Om Lay, Lillian wrote exactly what he said: "Gaoda and Gaodans are mentally and emotionally draining. I think I am in bad health." Management denied his form and requested a physical examination. Om Lay quit.

Lillian watched the townspeople wander around in their suits and dresses. During the meeting, they had lots of input on how to conduct the construction project. But all the construction workers Lillian worked with were from Shae town or near the inner city.

"It's a shame," Mrs. Silvers said. "We still have lots of work to do."

"Anything I can do?" Lillian said.

"Well, I have been working with a new communications director," Mrs. Silvers said. "We were thinking of a promotion project involving company families. Would you be interested?"

"What does that mean?"

"We'd take pictures of and have interviews with company families to promote the Grow in Gaoda expansion project," Mrs. Silvers explained. "We will make booklets and billboards."

"Billboards? I don't know—"

"They'd appear near construction sites. I think if people see your family they might want to get involved... since a lot of the workers like you."

"Oh. I don't know..." Lillian rubbed the back of her neck.

The workers did talk to Lillian more. Lillian thought it was because she understood them and because she was also from the inner city. The supervisors were Gaoda residents. They didn't understand the struggles of commuting from the inner city and were less lenient when they arrived late or had to leave early to pick up their kids from school. "Why can't they let their chauffer do it?" the senior coordinator had said.

"You would represent Gaoda well." Mrs. Silvers tapped her pointer finger on the table to get Lillian's attention.

"Can I think about it?" Lillian said.

The next day after the party, Mrs. Silvers' assistant met with Lillian to talk about the advertising project. She explained that they will do a photoshoot with Lillian's family. The photoshoot will be done in one day, and the staff would take care of the sets and styling. Then she told Lillian how much money she and Diego would receive. That number lingered in Lillian's mind throughout the day. She knew they could use it to fix their leaky showerhead or replace their freezer and dryer.

Lillian mentioned the project to her friends at the next townhall meeting.

"That's awesome!" Amy clapped her hands and pulled Lillian into a hug. "You can share your beautiful little family."

Mrs. Anderson nodded and said with a tight-lipped smile, "Glad you can get good opportunities like that. Mrs. Silvers is quite generous."

"Does that mean your face will be everywhere?" Amy patted Lillian's arm.

"Possibly," Lillian said and looked down. She felt heat rise in her face.

That night, she asked Diego about the project after dinner. They stood facing each other in their small kitchen.

"I'm not good on camera," Diego said.

"Not true." Lillian pouted and interlocked her hands with his, then swung them back and forth. "We can show off our family. We also need some new workers for the expansion project…"

"Is that what you want?" Diego caressed his thumb along the back of her hand.

"Mrs. Silvers could use the—"

"Not again." Diego released their hands. "You can't say no to that lady."

"Well." Lillian studied the countertops then pointed at their broken oven. "They will pay us well."

Diego sighed. They always needed extra money.

★

The following morning, Lillian visited Mrs. Silvers' office for lunch. Mrs. Silvers clapped her hands together in excitement because Lillian agreed that her family would be the faces for Grow in Gaoda advertisements.

After two phone calls, a communications director, advertising agents, interns, and a photographer piled into Mrs. Silvers' office. They gathered around Lillian on the couch.

"Wow, you have strong cheekbones," a young girl with short, pink hair and bright eyes said. Around her neck was a tag that read Emma: Marketing Intern. "You must have a pretty family."

Lillian smiled and tucked her hair back behind her ears.

The advertising staff asked for descriptions of Lillian's home and family. Lillian pulled out her wallet to show off her best family picture—a photo Clark took when Maria was four years old.

"Such a sweet face," the photographer said, examining the picture in Lillian's wallet. "We should go with a simple concept around a couple of sets."

"So, do I have to dress a certain way? Or…" Lillian played with her wallet.

"We'll take care of everything," Emma added.

On Sunday, a crew of stylists, set designers, and photographers arrived at the Luas' home in two black vans. They rolled out boxes of lighting equipment and set it up around their living room and kitchen.

Emma explained that they had three photoshoot concepts to finish that day. The first shoot was focused on the nuclear family, where the crew set up the living room with old appliances like a rotary phone and box tv. The stylist dressed Lillian in heels and a button-up flare dress. Diego joined her on the sofa, wearing a blue suit and a tie, and held a briefcase. Maria sat on the floor wearing a puffy dress and a large bow in her hair.

The second photo concept was inspired by storybooks. The crew decorated their old wooden fence with hanging flowers and set up a bench covered in stacks of books. Lillian and Maria wore light blue dresses with puffy sleeves, and Diego wore a white button-down. They sat on a grey blanket with an open book in front of them. They took photos of Maria playing outside until the sun started to set.

The third photo concept was a contemporary home scene. After the crew searched their house for a good spot, they decided to do the photoshoot in Maria's room. They shifted Maria's paper lanterns around onto one wall and set up lights on the other side. As they searched the house for extra props, they found an old white crib in the basement.

"Where's the baby?" Maria asked Diego, tiptoeing to look inside the crib.

"You will pretend to be a big sister," the director said.

"I'm a sister?" Maria exclaimed and jumped up and down.

"No, no," Diego said, patting her head.

"Uh, what's this concept?" Lillian turned to the director.

"This is a contemporary one," the director explained. "It would be good for the section on building new families."

"I am not pregnant," Lillian said.

On cue, Emma scurried over and handed Lillian a silicone baby belly. "Here you are."

"Well, you're going to pretend," the director said, waving at them to move towards the crib.

"I don't know if we should—" Diego started.

"Look," the photographer interjected. "This is the last shoot, and my crew's getting hungry. Can we just finish this?"

The Luas glanced at each other and nodded. Maria jumped up for Diego to pick her up. Lillian, Diego, and Maria stood behind the crib and looked down at it. Lillian stared at the empty spot.

"Don't forget to hold your stomach!" Emma called from the side.

"Look excited! Like you're expecting a baby!" The director lunged forward with his camera and snapped his fingers.

Lillian looked up at Maria, who was in Diego's arms. Maria played with a new doll the crew gave her. Lillian loosened her shoulders, rubbed her stomach, and held a small smile.

The cameras flashed like approaching car lights. In a blink, the crew scattered around the room, unplugged the lights, rolled up extension cords, and broke down the crib.

Maria frowned as they stuffed the play blocks, books, and dolls back into plastic boxes. Lillian walked out into the living room and watched two staff members pack the flowers on the lawn back onto a cart. The stylist zipped up the wardrobe and dropped it into more boxes and onto carts. They wheeled everything back out and loaded them into the black vans.

"Thank you for welcoming us into your home," Emma said to Lillian as she set a box of sandwiches on their kitchen counter. "You did great."

"Thank you." Lillian smiled and walked Emma out to the front porch and closed the door.

Lillian looked around their house again. The crew placed back their broken accordion blinds.

Clark visited the Luas on the weekends often when Maria was younger. On Sundays, Clark and Diego spent the day on the couch around the TV and a twenty-four-pack case of beer.

One night, Diego fell asleep at eight in the evening as Clark sat and surfed through channels on TV. When Lillian came home from attending a town committee meeting, she collapsed onto the sofa next to him. The coffee table was full of beer bottles, empty cans, and a half-eaten nacho tray.

"I'm not cleaning that." Lillian sighed.

"You got a package or something." Clark kicked at the seat where a thick, yellow envelope sat on top.

Lillian grabbed the envelope, opened it, and pulled out pictures from their family shoot: glossy photos of their unrecognizable home. Clark leaned over to look at them. Before Lillian could pull it away, he grabbed a handful of the pictures.

"What's this?" he laughed.

"I am helping Mrs. Silvers with advertising Gaoda." Lillian sat back.

"As a housewife?"

"They're concepts."

"So, you're showing a pretty version of your life," Clark said and held up the family photo of Lillian, Diego and Maria sitting around a box TV. "If I were the photographer, I'd focus on your reality."

"Well, you aren't," Lillian snapped.

"Is this what you want?" Clark said, slurring his words. He waved a photo of them standing around the stove, smiling. The words "look at this happy family" were scrawled across the top.

"I have everything I need," Lillian said.

"Nothing wrong with this," Clark laughed, sifting through the photos from the storybook scene. "It's your happily ever after."

"They're concepts." Lillian fidgeted with the photos from the shoot in Maria's bedroom. She examined them and noticed how the white crib glowed, and the soft lights from the paper lanterns made the walls look like a night sky.

Clark snatched the rest of the photos from Lillian's hand. "Grow in Gaoda," he read aloud. "Yeah, with this fake life."

"What's your problem?" Lillian crossed her arms.

"I guess I don't see you as a go-lucky housewife. You want all this stuff?"

"I'm not a sellout."

"I didn't say that." Clark smirked.

Lillian got up, grabbed two wine bottles off the coffee table, and poured them into the sink. Clark tried to lurch forward but fell back and shouted, "Ay Oun, you're so immature."

Lillian stormed down the hall then stopped when she saw Maria sitting on the floor outside her bedroom, hugging her knees. "*Mija?*" Lillian said.

"Ba didn't say goodnight," Maria whispered. "I couldn't sleep."

Lillian kissed Maria's head. "Let's go," she said as she scooped up Maria into her arms.

Chapter 9

The Neighbourhood Watch

When Maria was eight years old, Clark took Maria out to play on the edge of town, near the river and an abandoned highway. It was a quiet spot, unlike the Gaodan parks where there was always a runner, dog walker, or a group of teenagers wandering through the park. Unlike Penna City, Gaodans made eye contact with the strangers they passed by. They didn't smile back at Clark.

Clark and Maria sat on a grey blanket next to the rocks. Clark skipped stones while Maria searched for the shiny rocks that glittered in the moonlight.

It was nine o'clock in the evening, but Clark wanted Maria to see the night sky. When Clark and Maria drew stories together, Maria added stars to every page. When Clark left town last weekend, he took a wrong turn towards an abandoned highway. Before he turned around he noticed a river and a clear view of the night sky. He remembered the route so he could show Maria.

"From here, the stars look quite small," Clark explained. "But they're actually quite big."

"But my finger's bigger?" Maria held up her finger and pinched.

"They're far away, but when you're close, the stars are big and overwhelming," Clark said, pulling out a journal from his back pocket. "I should write that down."

"Another story?" Maria stood behind him and rested her chin on his shoulder.

"Maybe?" Clark laughed.

A circle of light fell onto his page. Clark turned around. A shadow waving a flashlight blinded his eyes.

"Maria should be asleep." Lillian stood over Clark.

"We were just watching the sunset." Clark slumped in the plastic chair. He crossed his arms as the vent blasted cold air above him.

They were in the Gaodan police station in the neighbourhood watch division. Colourful posters titled "Don't Talk to Strangers" and "Having some trouble? Call Neighbourhood watch!" covered the brick walls.

"I didn't know he was your brother," Amy said from behind them. "I wouldn't have reported him."

Lillian turned around. Amy's face appeared red, and she held her hands at her chest. Mrs. Anderson stood next to her, looking at her heels.

"From a distance, Maria was with someone…" Amy eyed Clark. "We didn't know and called Neighbourhood Watch. I am sorry."

Clark stared at his hands.

"Thank you for looking out for Maria," Lillian said. "It is an honest mistake."

Clark stood up. "Going to the bathroom," he said to the officer next to them. "That's okay, right?"

The officer nodded, and Clark disappeared down the hallway.

"That's your brother?" Mrs. Anderson said once he was out of sight.

"Yes," Lillian said, looking at her feet.

"He looks familiar. I think he's talked to my husband before." Mrs. Anderson turned to Lillian. "I just wanted you to know, he was also on private property. There will be fines."

Lillian nodded.

★

Lillian and Clark listened to the wheezing of the broken air conditioner in Lillian's used car. Lillian alternated which hand she placed on the wheel to wipe her sweat off on her jeans. Clark rested his head against the window.

"Those are your friends?" Clark finally spoke.

"They have been helpful when we first came to Gaoda," Lillian said.

"Wouldn't they know about me?"

"Well, you're not here often."

"Right."

"Mrs. Anderson mentioned you've been talking with her husband," Lillian said.

"The blonde lady is Mrs. Anderson?" Clark asked.

"Yeah…"

"I don't know."

"Okay," Lillian said. She was used to Clark breaking out into advice or criticism. He always had something to say to her. But he was more interested in the dashboard.

They didn't talk for the rest of the night and Clark left early Sunday morning.

★

After a town hall dinner, Mrs. Anderson pulled Lillian aside. They stood outside, behind the Gaodan city hall building.

"I looked further into what my husband said about your brother," Mrs. Anderson said. "We felt bad about calling the neighbourhood watch on him."

"What's this about?" Lillian settled herself on the back wall. It had been two weeks since the incident at the police station.

"He's a writer, yes?"

Lillian nodded.

"He has been asking around about the rezoning and expansion. Apparently, there are some legal issues with the expansion project," Mrs. Anderson said, eyeing the large open window to their side. "Mrs. Silvers didn't seem happy."

Lillian studied Mrs. Anderson's expression. Mrs. Anderson furrowed her brow, but her mouth twitched slightly.

"You think my brother is involved?" Lillian said.

Mrs. Anderson nodded.

★

Lillian planned to ask Clark about his involvement with the expansion project the next weekend. If it were true, Lillian wasn't sure what to do. Lillian talked to the management of the expansion project and Mrs. Silvers' assistant to find press request information. There was an array of safety claims and unmet zoning laws.

Clark's name was included on interview request forms as a journalist interviewing Mrs. Silvers. There were rumors of an investigation into the Silvers family and the expansion project.

"So, they're doing background checks on me?" Clark crossed his arms. They sat across from each other at the kitchen table.

"They just mentioned you might be part of the investigation," Lillian said. "That would delay a lot of our work and…"

"They should just leave the district alone."

"If you drop the story—" Lillian started.

"Are you their yes man or something?" Clark pointed his finger.

"Clark." Lillian slumped her shoulders. "Gaodans are influential."

"So, I should just take their money and keep quiet?" Clark said.

"I can help through my job...maybe talk to people in Shae town." Lillian twisted her necklace pendant. "I could keep my job..."

"And what about my job?" Clark said. "Aren't you the least bit worried about the people in Shae town?"

"Of course." Lillian stopped fiddling with her necklace.

"I think you forgot where you came from." Clark stood up and walked away.

Lillian and Clark began talking through Diego. Whenever she and Clark talked, the conservation went in circles. Diego relayed messages from Lillian to drop the story. Clark didn't.

"They blacklisted him," Diego told Lillian at the kitchen table. "He has to avoid Gaoda for now."

"Maybe it's for the best," Lillian said.

Once Clark went to the police station, it wasn't long until more townspeople discovered he was related to Lillian. Then they learned he was part of the campaign against Gaoda. When Lillian last walked along the construction site fences that lined an abandoned lot, she noticed graffiti covering the Grow in Gaoda advertisements. They scribbled out faces and replaced the slogans with the words "fake family."

Diego grabbed Lillian's hand. "They will probably ask you questions," he said.

"I have to help the town however I can," Lillian said.

"And Clark?"

Chapter 10

A Better Life

Lillian opens the front door. It takes her a moment to recognize Farren Silvers.

"Mrs. Lua." Farren bows her head. "It's been a while," Farren says. She was now eighteen years old and tall. She wore her signature shiny, strawberry blonde hair in a medium lob.

"Maria's not home," Lillian says.

"Oh, I thought she would be home by now." Farren rubs the back of her neck. "I guess I should have called?"

"Is everything okay?"

"We haven't talked in a while…but when I heard she might be leaving…I thought I should come by…" Farren says, rocking on her feet.

"Leaving…" Lillian says, tilting her head. "You mean the college tours? Aren't you a part of that?"

"What's that?"

"Maria went to tour campuses over March break."

"Oh? I heard she was catching a bus towards Shae or Penna …" Farren mumbles. "I guess I'll come back. Could you give this to her?" Farren hands her a sticky note, then smiles. "Nice to see you."

"Thank you, say hello to your Grandma," Lillian says. Then looks down at the note:

Hey little one, here is my new number! Call me.

★

"News travels fast," Diego says later that day, placing another gift basket on the kitchen table for Lillian.

Lillian opens it. It is a note from Amy that says:

It's been so long! Wish I could see you! Sad to know you're thinking of leaving. We will miss you.

"The Silvers have some power," Diego says.

"I don't think this was Farren," Lillian says. "She just wanted to see Maria."

"Either way, there's a lot of goodbye gifts and notes. Are they eager for us to leave?" Diego laughs and nudges Lillian's shoulder.

"Is this what you want, *mija*?" Lillian says to herself, thinking about Maria.

★

Later that day, Lillian wanders into Maria's bedroom to grab her laundry basket and stays to clean up Maria's desk. Balled-up sketches were stuffed in Maria's drawers. At the bottom of the drawer is a folder of college applications, fund request forms, and a scholarship rejection letter. More than one scholarship rejection letter.

Behind the letters was a "Better Life" scholarship information page. Maria drew a star next to three passages:

Eligible for ALL students. Inner-city and racialized students encouraged to apply.

Strong candidates must come from a family working in the county, volunteers, attends main fundraisers, and has a clean police record.

Make connections, make careers. Growing success for the soon-to-be-successful.

Mrs. Silvers used those words to describe the Luas. She said the Luas had promise. But Lillian had worked in the same position for sixteen years.

Since Clark opened an investigation on the Gaoda's expansion projects, he unlocked a slew of investigation claims. Lillian spent extra time with the communications and public relations team helping them sift through the evidence and dispute claims.

Every townsperson she talked to had told her not to worry. They found no problems with how the construction projects would uproot families and businesses in the Shae town because it was a "run-down ghost town."

The marketing communications team collected Clark's research, writing, and accusations, which Lillian volunteered to review. She found out Clark interviewed older workers about the construction site conditions, the management, and the expectations. In his chicken-scratch handwriting, he wrote: *Is Gaoda redlining? Is Gaoda co-opting land and kicking out more low-income neighbourhoods? Is Gaoda taking over the inner city?*

Lillian could hear him saying "how are you apart of this, Lil?" in his self-righteous tone. Lillian sometimes caught herself wishing he would say it to her. Instead, he left.

Lillian walks over to Maria's bed and lies down. On the ceiling, the glow-in-the-dark stars are now faded. Maria's dark blue bedroom was the only room that could calm Maria down when she was a little girl. They haven't changed her room in eighteen years. When Lillian and Diego repainted the house in eggshell white, they planned to repaint Maria's room, but she refused.

"The colour's a little dark," Lillian had said.

"But I like it," eight-year-old Maria had replied. "I feel like I am sitting under the night sky. It's calming."

Maria was right.

Lillian had checked her phone throughout the week, waiting for Maria to call. Maria sent back a few short texts like "at the hotel," "busy now," or "phone dead. Talk soon."

"I should be more worried," Lillian says to herself, rubbing her collar bone.

When Lillian complained to Diego about their daughters sparse messaging, Diego admitted he received a text from Clark. Clark messaged that Maria was staying with him for March break. Lillian should feel upset with Clark and Maria but as she stared at

Maria's star-speckled ceiling, all she thought about was seeing her brother again.

★

Lillian requests a meeting with Mrs. Silvers for the last day of March Break. For a few months, Mrs. Silvers was out of town, looking for new investors and spaces to own as part of Growing in Gaoda. She and Lillian hadn't talked like they used to since Clark opened up disputes against her.

Lillian had scrambled to keep the project together for her, but Diego reminded Lillian there was only so much she could do.

"You're not responsible for what other people do," Diego said.

"What will she think? I must seem so ungrateful," Lillian said.

"Maybe she had this coming."

The last time Lillian mentioned working somewhere else, Mrs. Silver shot it down.

"We have so much to do. You want to leave in the middle of it?" Mrs. Silvers said.

"There is always so much to do," Lillian wanted to say, but she said "I know" instead.

"How was your trip?" Lillian asks Mrs. Silvers when she enters Mrs. Silvers' office.

"Fine." Mrs. Silvers sits with her legs crossed over the other at her desk. Her elbows on the table and fingers touching.

"I've actually been meaning to talk to you…" Lillian says as she walks in front of the couch.

Mrs. Silvers nods for her to sit and says, "I don't have much time right now. Can we make it quick?"

"Oh, well, uh…" Lillian says. "I was thinking…I might explore new jobs."

"Now?" Mrs. Silvers stops moving her fingers. "You know how—"

"Busy it is," Lillian finishes Mrs. Silvers' sentence. "Yes, it will always be busy. But I could find people who could fulfill my duties and take care of things."

"Have you thought this through?" Mrs. Silvers says.

"It's just something I've been considering." Lillian looks down. "I thought I should be honest with you, and I am grateful—"

"But you would abandon your work? You had a lot of promise."

"Then why have I been in the same position for sixteen years?" Lillian says.

Mrs. Silvers crosses her arms. "You're complaining now?"

"I have spent so much time working..." Lillian says, studying the ground, "towards a temporary home."

"So, you came here today to delay my project again?" Mrs. Silvers says.

"I can help find you someone." Lillian steadies her hands on the couch and shifts forward.

"Time's up." The assistant knocks on their door.

"This is not how I expected my day to go." Mrs. Silvers stands up and walks towards her assistant. "Find the resignation request forms for Mrs. Lua here," she says, then walks out the door.

Lillian stays on the couch and listens as the clicking of Mrs. Silvers' heels fade down the hallway.

Chapter 11

Penna City

Maria sidesteps the chalk drawings on the pavement, careful not to ruin the rainbows, stick figures, and flowers. The night before, Clark requested to take the rest of the week off of work so that he and Maria could tour the colleges and he could show her the city. They walk downtown past the novelty shops, convenience stores, and small restaurants.

Clark leads Maria past alleyways full of murals towards his old apartment. Since he often travelled for work, he rented an apartment short-term for three to four months at a time. His landlord, Silvia Perez, was friends with his grandmother, Yey Chan. But he does not call her Silvia, she tells him to call her *Abuelita*, meaning "grandmother" in Spanish.

"*Oun*." Abuelita smiles at Clark. *Oun* refers to a younger relative or friend in Khmer. Yey Chan taught Abuelita Spanish, and Abuelita taught Yey Chan how to speak Khmer.

"This is my niece." Clark ruffles the top of Maria's head.

Maria's height lands just above his shoulder. It took Clark a few days to comfortably pat Maria's head again. When he reached out, she smiled and nodded at him to let him know it was okay.

Abuelita holds her hands out towards Maria.

"Hello." Maria bows and takes her hand. They feel soft.

"You look just like your mother." Abuelita smiles and pats the top of Maria's hand. "Hope she is okay?"

"She is well," Maria says, trying to maintain Abuelita's intense eye contact.

"Tell her I am getting old." Abuelita shakes her head. "I might forget her face soon. She must come by."

"I will tell her," Maria says and allows Abuelita to pat her hands a little longer.

Abuelita hands Clark the keys to the rooftop doorway. They had trouble with the neighbourhood kids drinking, smoking, and trashing up the rooftop, so Abuelita had to install a lock. Maria walks around the flowerpots, lawn chairs, and white, plastic, foldable tables. She leans on the brick ledge railing as she gazes at the city.

"I feel like I've seen this view before," Maria says.

"I think I gave your dad a picture of this," Clark says, remembering it on Diego's wall when he first visited Lillian and Diego. They took it down when they repainted the house white and replaced it with a mirror.

"It's nice." Maria tilts her head, watching the sunlight reflect off the glass windows.

The street view is colourful, from the different coloured shops and the patterns in the alleyway murals.

Clark watches Maria take in the view. "I wish I brought my camera," he says.

She looks at her uncle and reaches into her jean pocket for her phone.

"No, it's not the same." Clark shakes his head.

"Not professional enough?" Maria laughs.

"Just come to the city again. I'll bring my camera," Clark says.

Maria smiles as she rests her elbows on the ledge and places her chin in her hands. "So, this is where you and Ma grew up?"

"We played up here a lot with the neighbour kids," Clark says. "When it was just us, we fought a little too much. We don't always agree on everything. Yey wouldn't let us leave the rooftop until we made up."

Maria still hadn't asked Clark about what happened between Lillian and him.

"I don't always agree with Ma either," Maria says. "When I want to talk to her, I wait until she's not tired, but she's usually…she works a lot."

"Lillian's not one to quit things," Clark says. "She wouldn't leave her warehouse work here, but she complained about it all the time. I don't think she would have left the city if she hadn't gotten pregnant with you." Clark turns to look at Maria.

Maria's eyes fixate on the rooftop of a building below them where kids play.

"I think you gave her lots of hope, though," Clark adds.

Maria looks back at Clark. She notices the fine lines under his eyes.

"She left Penna to find something better." He looks back at the city. "But I don't know if she found it."

★

On Saturday, Clark and Maria spend their last day together before Maria has to take the bus back home. Abuelita invites them over so she could send her signature tamales home with Maria. When they arrive, the doorman tells them to go to the rooftop.

"Abuelita?" Clark says as he opens the door to the roof.

"*Aqui*," Over here, Abuelita says in Spanish. She ushers them over to a patio table where she sits next to Lillian. Plates of tamales, and chicken and rice cover the table.

"I didn't know where you were staying," Lillian says as Clark and Maria take their seats.

"How did you—what are you doing here?" Maria says, avoiding her mother's eyes.

"I came to pick you up. I told Diego to tell you I was coming." Lillian looks at Clark. Lillian had rehearsed what to say to them the entire car ride, but with Abuelita there, she decides to save the conversation for later.

"That's good. The bus rides are long," Clark says, studying his hands.

"Is there something wrong with my food?" Abuelita interjects, handing Clark and Maria a fork. "Eat up."

Abuelita asks Lillian and Maria about Diego, Gaoda, jobs, and colleges. Clark listens as Lillian does the most talking, and Maria answers a question ever so often. They talk until the sun sets and Abuelita needs to sleep.

"I can't stay up like we used to." Abuelita stands up and hands keys to Clark. "Lock up when you're done, and don't forget to take food home."

"Yes, Abuelita," Lillian and Clark say in unison.

Abuelita takes Maria's hand and pats the top of her hand. "If only your Yey could see you." She smiles, then leans in for a hug and whispers, "give them space to talk things out. They both have a lot of pride."

Abuelita pulls away, smiles and says, "goodnight, my dear."

"Goodnight, Abuelita." Maria smiles and nods.

Lillian and Clark remain silent and watch her leave.

"I am glad you are well." Clark breaks the silence and looks at Lillian. "I think Abuelita was really happy to see you."

"Yes," Lillian says. "I am happy to see Abuelita too."

Their eyes meet.

"It's getting late," Clark says. "Why don't you stay the night and leave tomorrow?"

★

"Your kitchen is so messy," Lillian tells Clark in the morning.

Lillian and Maria slept in Clark's bed while he slept on the couch. He woke up early and had trouble going back to sleep, so he went to the kitchen, made coffee, and caught up on his work. Notebooks scatter across the countertop.

"There's more coffee if you want." Clark points to the kettle and coffee beans near the stove.

"Thank you." Lillian grabs a mug and spoon from the sink and prepares a cup of coffee.

"What you were saying to Abuelita last night...are you really doing okay?" Clark says, playing with the pencil in his hand.

"What do you think, Bong?" Lillian stirs her coffee and watches it spin in the cup. "I've been rethinking things...I want to be mad at you, but..."

"Well, I pushed you. I just wanted those Gaodans to stop walking around the inner city and taking it all,"

Clark says, rubbing his arm. "It was frustrating to see you be a part of it like you were forgetting—"

"Where I am from."

"You were just doing your job."

Lillian sips her coffee and stares at the countertop. "When Diego told me Maria came here, all I could think about was what you would think of me," Lillian says. "I was glad you left because then you wouldn't see me spend all this time…trying so hard to stay in Gaoda."

"You wanted a good life for Maria."

"But is it any better than if she were living here?"

"I don't know."

"I left my job," Lillian says, tapping her cup. "Maria's going to college soon and will need the money. Maybe I can find a better-paying job to help her…"

A thud comes from the hallway. Clark and Lillian turn around. Maria lurches forward to pick up the phone she dropped on the floor.

"Someone's nosy." Clark chuckles.

"I just got up," Maria says, holding her phone to her chest. "I heard nothing."

"Right," Clark says.

"I'm glad you're talking." Maria walks up and slides into the seat next to Clark.

"Thanks, kid." Clark reaches out to pat the hair behind the back of her neck.

Clark and Maria share a smile. Lillian walks up to them at the counter.

"But you also snuck out to the city." Lillian leans forward and presses her forehead to Maria's. "Don't think I forgot that."

Chapter 12

Donation Boxes

Maria crosses her legs on her bed, twirling the sticky note her mom gave her between her fingers. On the sticky note, in thin writing, a memo reads:

Hey little one, here is my new number! Call me.

Only Farren called her "little one" as a term of endearment. Her classmates, especially Remy, joked about Maria's height. When Farren stopped walking with her after school six years ago, they only talked when they passed each other in the hallways.

Maria picks up her phone, texts "hello", then sets her phone down. After a few seconds, the phone rings.

"Hello?" Maria says.

"Hey," Farren's soft voice answers.

"Why'd you call?" Maria plays with the note in her hands.

"You texted me," Farren says.

"Well, I got your note."

"Yeah, your mom said you were looking at colleges. Isn't it a little early to look?" Farren says. "I always thought you'd go to Gaodan College like the rest of us."

"And copy you?" Maria laughs.

"No, I think you could do something better," Farren laughs. "Like drawing…you'd be good at that."

"Thank you." Maria smiles. She didn't think Farren noticed.

"I miss your voice. Are you really leaving?"

"We are thinking about it…but I'm still here for now," Maria says. "We can walk together after school tomorrow?"

"I drive now," Farren laughs. "So, how about I pick you up?"

★

Diego, Lillian, and Maria sit on a picnic blanket on their cold, stone basement floor. They spent the morning cleaning up the kitchen and living room, took a lunch break, then moved to the basement in the afternoon.

Maria takes CDs out of a box, and Lillian sorts them into different piles. Diego takes CDs from her pile to test them in the CD player to see if they still play. Then, he stops sorting through items and sing. He stands up to start dancing to "Smooth" by Santana and Rob Thomas, but he has to crouch because of the low ceilings.

"Ah!" Diego says and grabs his elbow that just hit against the shelf behind him.

"We actually thought we could make this your play-room," Lillian laughs.

"Really?" Maria looks up at the exposed wood and wires on the ceiling. "I think I'd be scared down here."

"Well, we were going to get it finished," Diego says, sitting back down on the blanket.

"We were going to put in soft lights and shelves." Lillian points at the ceiling and brought her hand down to the wall. "Clark was going to paint you a forest scene with animals."

"That would've been nice," Maria says, sitting back on her hands and looking at the wall. The framed photos that Clark took of Penna City hang on the wall.

Once Maria arrived home from Penna, she searched the basement for all of Clark's photos. She found pictures of the cityscape, strangers waiting on buses, standing by corner stores, or walking through the city. Clark explained to Maria that he liked to get both views of the city: up close and distant. He said seeing things from different angles gives a person a different perspective.

"If only Maria left her room," Diego says as he nudges Maria and hands her a box of used books to organize.

"Hey, I liked my room," Maria says. "I pretended I was sitting in space." She opens up the box and sorts through books and journals.

Lillian reaches forward when she sees the purple stapled book that Maria and Clark wrote together.

"You kept asking for a tiger after this story," Lillian says, running her hands along the crayon drawings. "You got upset when I wouldn't read this."

"Hey, I liked my stories too." Maria smiles and stacks books into piles. Her donate pile of books stacks higher than her keep pile.

"You're not keeping those books?" Diego pats the back of her head, looking at her piles.

"I think other people could use it," Maria says, taking back the book in Lillian's hand. "I'll keep the ones important to me."

Lillian looks at Maria. Maria hums to Santana's guitar solo while folding her old clothes before placing them into the donation boxes. Lillian smiles. Maria used to have trouble separating herself from her old toys. Diego joked that she got the fear of changing or leaving things from Lillian. Whenever he brought up the idea of leaving Gaoda, Lillian said no because Maria didn't even want to leave her room. Maria was Lillian's excuse.

"What?" Maria says, meeting her mother's eyes. "Do you want me to put these back?"

Lillian shakes her head. "No, no, we don't need those."

"We don't need these either," Diego says and slides a box of old baby clothes into the donate section.

"But these are cute." Lillian leans over and picks up a small white boxy dress.

"And who will use that?" Diego says.

"Maria might need them in the future for her kids…" Lillian twirls the hanger around and smiles.

"Uh…" Maria stops folding the clothes.

"Not anytime soon." Diego grabs the hanger and pulls it away from Lillian, then points at Maria. "College first, *mija*."

"She's not a kid anymore," Lillian teases as she hooks her arm with Diego's left arm and rests her head on his shoulder. Lillian pulls him side to side and says, "If we move to the city, and Maria goes to college, she might meet someone nice, like how we met, and…"

"Don't get too ahead of yourself, Ma," Maria laughs and sits on Diego's right side, links her arms with his, and leans her head onto Diego's shoulders.

Lillian laces her hands with Maria's. The CD scratches to a stop in the middle of a song, but no one gets up to fix it. Lillian and Maria close their eyes and listen to Diego hum the rest of the song.

Acknowledgements

Thank you to Life Rattle Press and Professor Guy Allen for making this book possible. This has been a valuable learning experience and I have connected with such an amazing writing community through the PWC program. I am grateful to have your guidance and support throughout this bookmaking process.

Endless thanks to my editor, Jessica Gelar. You have been incredibly helpful, kind, patient and I can go on and on. You've been instrumental in shaping this story. I am fortunate to have collaborated with you.

Deepest gratitude to my editing group: Danica, Kriti and Vanessa. You are an amazing, encouraging, and inspiring group of writers and editors. Thank you for all your support.

Shoutout to my UTM Scribes Slate team: Gladys, Natalie and Rhea. You have been major cheerleaders throughout this process. Thank you for lifting my confidence and spending late evenings listening to me go slightly crazy.

To my dear friends: Aryanna, Lenna, and Paige. I'll keep it simple: thanks. Okay I should make this acknowledgement a little bit longer, since you've spent so much time supporting me through the all-nighters, guiding me when I get indecisive and reminding me to get sleep (even though I don't listen). Special thanks to Aryanna for the input and help on the cover design. Thank you for everything.

Lastly, to my family: I appreciate your patience and care through the plates of fresh-cut strawberries you slide to me as I spend my days writing and editing. I am struggling to find a statement less cliché than, "I couldn't do this without you." Without you, I might've kept these stories to myself.

About the Author

Jenefer Savoeung is a University of Toronto graduate from the Professional Writing and Communication, Culture & Information Technology program. During her undergraduate days, she was an editor for Mind-waves & Compass, a writer for UTSC The Hub and the Co-Editor-in-Chief of UTM Scribes for Slate VI. Her article "Empty Rice Pots: Cambodian Refugees' Experiences with Food Insecurity" will be published in *Compass, Volume 8*.

When Jenefer is not writing or editing, she watches TV shows for "research" on storytelling or creates characters with in-depth backstories on *The Sims*. You can find her on Twitter @jens_write when she should be sleeping.

www.ingramcontent.com/pod-product-compliance
Lightning Source LLC
Chambersburg PA
CBHW030348180626
46812CB00007B/2811